D0547906

The Rainbow book

of Nursery Rhymes

A L I S
1598855

Sam Childs

RED FOX

ABERDEENSHIRE
LIBRARY &
INFORMATION SERVICES

WITHDRAWN
FROM LIBRARY

For Rufus David Pitt,

my gorgeous grandson

Childs, Sam

The rainbow book
of nursery
rhymes /
                    J398.
                      8
1598855

THE RAINBOW BOOK OF NURSERY RHYMES
A RED FOX BOOK 0 09 945112 3

First published in Great Britain by Hutchinson,
an imprint of Random House Children's Books

Hutchinson edition published 2001
Red Fox edition published 2004

1 3 5 7 9 10 8 6 4 2

Copyright © Sam Childs, 2001

The right of Sam Childs to be identified as the author and illustrator of this work has been asserted
in accordance with the Copyright, Designs and Patents Act 1988.

All rights reserved. No part of this publication may be reproduced, stored in a retrieval system, or transmitted
in any form or by any means, electronic, mechanical, photocopying, recording or otherwise,
without the prior permission of the publishers.

Red Fox Books are published by Random House Children's Books,
61–63 Uxbridge Road, London W5 5SA,
a division of The Random House Group Ltd,
in Australia by Random House Australia (Pty) Ltd,
20 Alfred Street, Milsons Point, Sydney, NSW 2061, Australia,
in New Zealand by Random House New Zealand Ltd,
18 Poland Road, Glenfield, Auckland 10, New Zealand,
and in South Africa by Random House (Pty) Ltd,
Endulini, 5A Jubilee Road, Parktown 2193, South Africa

THE RANDOM HOUSE GROUP Limited Reg. No. 954009
www.**kids**at**random**house.co.uk

A CIP catalogue record for this book is available from the British Library.

Printed in China

Contents

Foreword

by Sam Childs

I have always loved nursery rhymes. They are full of surreal situations and extraordinary characters that fire the imagination and make you laugh. As a child, I longed, like cow, to jump over the moon, or go round it like Sally on a Saturday afternoon. I wanted to know all the answers. Why did Terence McDiddler play his fiddle by the sea? Why did the old woman live in a shoe? And not only why was Joan jumping, but why was she all alone? As an adult I realized that these unsolved mysteries formed a wonderful basis for storytelling.

Nursery rhymes are a remnant of an oral tradition that goes back for centuries; many rhymes have their roots in political and historical situations that have long lost their meaning. Yet parents and grandparents continue to sing them to children and the rhymes are repeated and repeated until they are learned by heart. Most children can sing 'Twinkle, twinkle, little star' and 'Baa, baa, black sheep' long before they can string together a coherent sentence. As a small child, my son wept when we had to return Brian Wildsmith's wonderful *Mother Goose* (Oxford, 1964) to the library. I remember my mother singing 'Dance to your daddy' to him when he was very small and later he joined in with 'Diddle, diddle, dumpling', delighting in its alliteration. My daughter now sings the rhymes she learned as a child to her own son and has added some new ones to her repertoire.

Some of the rhymes in this book will be less familiar than others, but I hope that these will be memorised and passed on to a new generation. I have included the wonderful 'It's going to rain now, little Polly' by Christian Morgenstern, generously translated from the German by my niece Lorna Forte. You will also find a song about Itchy Coo, the squirrel, which was taught to me by a school friend Susan Anderson. I have no idea where she learned it because despite exhaustive enquiries, no one else seems to have heard of it. And some of the words on these pages may not be quite as you remember them. That's because they are as *I* remember them; you can alter them as you wish to make them a part of your family's rhymes.

During the process of selecting these rhymes, I have rediscovered some extraordinary books and seen some new ones. What a daunting prospect to be adding to the likes of *Lavender's Blue*, compiled by Kathleen Lines and illustrated by Harold Jones (Oxford, 1954) and *The Mother Goose Treasury*, illustrated by Raymond Briggs (Hamish Hamilton, 1966).

The making of this book has given me enormous pleasure. I hope the happiness I have experienced while painting these pictures will in some way communicate itself to you. Working around Inge Willems's stunning page designs has been both challenging and stimulating. A final thank you goes to my granddaughter, Clunie, for her indispensable colour sense and equanimity, which enabled me to finish the front cover when I was completely stuck.

Sam Childs, aged 41/2

Little Ones

Riddle: I'm called by the name of a man,
   Yet am as little as a mouse;
   When winter comes I love to be
   With my red target near the house.

Answer: A robin

Monday's child is fair of face,
Tuesday's child is full of grace,
Wednesday's child is full of woe,
Thursday's child has far to go,
Friday's child is loving and giving,
Saturday's child works hard for its living,
But the child that's born on the Sabbath day
Is bonny and wise and good and gay.

Hector Protector was dressed all in green,
Hector Protector was sent to the Queen;
The Queen did not like him,
No more did the King;
So Hector Protector was sent back again.

It's going to rain now, little Polly,
So hurry open up your brolly.

So hurry open up your brolly,
And hold tight to the handle, Polly.

And hold tight to the handle, Polly,
And run and run and run, by golly!

And run and run and run, by golly,
Until you find Shopkeeper Jolly.

Find the jolly man and say:
Good day to you – Good day! Good day!

Shopkeeper Jolly, just for fun,
Please may I have a piece of sun?

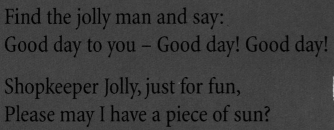

Please may I have a piece of sun,
To dry my brolly as I run,

To dry my brolly as I run –
And jolly man, he gets you one.

4

And he laughs because it's funny,
And brings a piece of sun so sunny.

And brings a piece of sun so sunny,
Doesn't it look like golden honey?

Like golden honey in paper bound,
And Mr Jolly wraps it round.

And Mr Jolly wraps it round
For you to bring home, safe and sound.

And when we open, all is sunny,
Doesn't it look like golden honey?

Then you get half, my little Polly
And half to dry your lovely brolly.

It's going to rain now, little Polly,
So run and run and run, by golly.

by Christian Morgenstern, translated by Lorna Forte

Little Blue Ben, who lives in the glen,

Keeps a blue cat and one blue hen,

Which lays of blue eggs a score and ten;

Where shall I find the little Blue Ben?

Little Boy Blue,
Come blow your horn,
The sheep's in the meadow,
The cow's in the corn;
But where is the boy
Who looks after the sheep?
He's under a haycock,
Fast asleep.

Little Bo-Peep has lost her sheep,
And doesn't know where to find them;
Leave them alone, and they'll come home,
Bringing their tails behind them.

Little Bo-Peep fell fast asleep,
And dreamed she heard them bleating;
But when she awoke, she found it a joke,
For they were still a-fleeting.

Then she took her little crook,
Determined for to find them;
She found them indeed, but it made her heart bleed
For they'd left all their tails behind them.

It happened one day, as Bo-Peep did stray
Into a meadow hard by;
There she espied their tails, side by side,
All hung on a tree to dry.

She heaved a sigh and wiped her eye,
And ran over hill and dale-o;
And tried what she could, as a shepherdess should
To fix to each sheep its tail-o.

9

Mary had a little lamb,
Its fleece was white as snow;
And everywhere that Mary went
The lamb was sure to go.

It followed her to school one day,
Which was against the rules;
It made the children laugh and play
To see a lamb at school.

And so the teacher turned it out,
But still it lingered near,
And waited patiently about
Till Mary did appear.

What makes the lamb love Mary so?
The eager children cry;
Why, Mary loves the lamb, you know,
The teacher did reply.

Little Miss Muffet
Sat on a tuffet,
Eating her curds and whey;
There came a big spider,
Who sat down beside her
And frightened Miss Muffet away.

Jack Hall,
He is so small,
A mouse could eat him,
Hat and all.

Jack and Jill went up the hill
To fetch a pail of water;
Jack fell down and broke his crown,
And Jill came tumbling after.

Then up Jack got and home did trot,
As fast as he could caper;
He went to bed to mend his head
With vinegar and brown paper.

Here I am, little Jumping Joan;
When nobody's with me,
I'm all alone.

Jeremiah Obadiah, puff, puff, puff,
When he gives his messages, he snuffs, snuffs, snuffs,
When he goes to school by day, he roars, roars, roars,
When he goes to bed at night, he snores, snores, snores,
When he goes to Christmas treat, he eats plum-duff,
Jeremiah Obadiah, puff, puff, puff.

Anna Maria, she sat on the fire,
The fire was too hot, she sat on the pot,
The pot was too round, she sat on the ground,
The ground was too flat, she sat on the cat,
The cat ran away with Maria on her back.

I love little pussy,
Her coat is so warm,
And if I don't hurt her
She'll do me no harm;
So I'll not pull her tail,
Nor drive her away,
But pussy and I
Very gently will play.

19

Three little kittens they lost their mittens
And they began to cry,
Oh, mother dear, we sadly fear
That we have lost our mittens.
What! Lost your mittens, you naughty kittens!
Then you shall have no pie.
Mee-ow, mee-ow, mee-ow,
No, you shall have no pie.

Three little kittens they found their mittens,
And they began to cry,
Oh, mother dear, see here, see here,
For we have found our mittens.
Put on your mittens, you silly kittens,
And you shall have some pie.
Purr-r, purr-r, purr-r,
Oh, let us have some pie.

Three little kittens put on their mittens,
And soon ate up the pie;
Oh, mother dear, we greatly fear
That we have soiled our mittens.
What! Soiled your mittens, you naughty kittens!
Then they began to sigh,
Mee-ow, mee-ow, mee-ow,
Then they began to sigh.

The three little kittens they washed their mittens,
And hung them out to dry;
Oh, mother dear, do you not hear
That we have washed our mittens?
What! Washed your mittens, then you're good kittens,
But I smell a rat close by.
Mee-ow, mee-ow, mee-ow,
We smell a rat close by.

23

Five little pussy cats sitting in a row,

Blue ribbons round each neck, fastened in a bow;

Hey pussies! Ho pussies! Are your faces clean?

Don't you know you're sitting there so as to be seen?

There was a little dog and he had a little tail,
And he used to wag, wag, wag it!
But when he was sad, because he had been bad,
On the ground he would drag, drag, drag it!

Oh where, oh where
has my little dog gone?
Oh where, oh where
can he be?

With his ears cut short
and his tail cut long,
Oh where, oh where is he?

26

Tom, Tom, the piper's son
Stole a pig and away did run;
The pig was eat
And Tom was beat,
And Tom went howling down the street.

Diddle, diddle, dumpling, my son John,
Went to bed with his trousers on;
One shoe off, and one shoe on,
Diddle, diddle, dumpling, my son John.

Dance to your daddy,
my little babby,
Dance to your daddy,
my little lamb;
You shall have a fishy
in a little dishy,
You shall have a fishy
when the boat comes in.

29

Bye, baby bunting,

Daddy's gone a-hunting,

Gone to get a rabbit skin

To wrap his baby bunting in.

Fun and Games

What is orange?
Why, an orange,
Just an orange!

How many days has my baby to play?
Saturday, Sunday, Monday,
Tuesday, Wednesday, Thursday, Friday,
Saturday, Sunday, Monday.
Hop away, skip away,
My baby wants to play,
My baby wants to play every day!

Round and round the garden
Like a teddy bear;
One step, two step,
Tickle you under there!

Here we go round the mulberry bush,
The mulberry bush, the mulberry bush;
Here we go round the mulberry bush,
All on a frosty morning.

This is the way we clap our hands,
Clap our hands, clap our hands;
This is the way we clap our hands,
All on a frosty morning.

This is the way we wash our clothes,
Wash our clothes, wash our clothes;
This is the way we wash our clothes,
All on a frosty morning.

Here we come gathering nuts in May,
Nuts in May, nuts in May;
Here we come gathering nuts in May
On a cold and frosty morning.

Who will you have for nuts in May,
Nuts in May, nuts in May;
Who will you have for nuts in May
On a cold and frosty morning?

Here we go looby loo,
Here we go looby light;
Here we go looby loo,
All on a Saturday night.

Put your right hand in,

Put your right hand out,

Shake it a little, a little,

And turn yourself about.

In and out the dusty bluebells,
In and out the dusty bluebells,
In and out the dusty bluebells,
Who shall be your master?

Tippa, tippa, tap upon your shoulder,
Tippa, tippa, tap upon your shoulder,
Tippa, tippa, tap upon your shoulder,
I shall be your master!

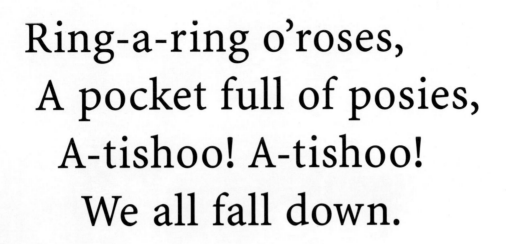

Ring-a-ring o'roses,
A pocket full of posies,
A-tishoo! A-tishoo!
We all fall down.

Boys and girls come out to play,
The moon doth shine as bright as day;

Leave your supper and leave your sleep,
And join your playfellows in the street.

Come with a whoop and come with a call,
Come with a good will or not at all;

Up the ladder and down the wall,
A half-penny loaf will serve us all.

Sally go round
the sun,

Sally go round
the moon,

Sally go round
the chimneypots,

On a Saturday
afternoon.

45

See-saw, Margery Daw,
Johnny shall have a new master;
He shall have but a penny a day,
Because he can't go any faster.

How much wood would a wood-chuck chuck
If a wood-chuck could chuck wood?
He would chuck as much wood
As a wood-chuck would chuck,
If a wood-chuck could chuck wood.

In a cottage in a wood,
A little old man by the window stood,
Saw a rabbit running by,
Knocking at his door.

Help me! Help me! the rabbit said,
Before the farmer shoots me dead! ...BANG
Come, little rabbit, stay with me,
And happy you will be!

49

Down by the river
    where the green grass grows,
Pretty Polly Perkins
    washes her clothes.
She sings, she sings,
    she sings so sweet;

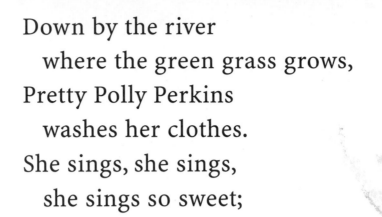

She sings for her true love,
  across the street.
He kissed her, he kissed her,
  he took her to the town;
He bought her a ring,
  and a fine silk gown.

This little pig
had a rub-a-dub,

This little pig
had a scrub-a-scrub,

This little pig-a-wig
ran upstairs,

This little pig-a-wig
called out, Bears!

Down came the jar
with a loud SLAM! SLAM!

And this little pig
had all the jam.

52

Incy Wincy spider
Climbing up the spout;
Down came the rain
And washed the spider out;
Out came the sunshine
And dried up all the rain;
Incy Wincy spider
Climbing up again.

Do your ears
hang low?

Do they wobble
to and fro?

Can you tie them
in a knot?

54

Can you tie them
in a bow?

Can you throw them
over your shoulder,
Like a regimental soldier?

Do your ears hang low?

55

A sailor went to sea, sea, sea,
To see what he could see, see, see;

But all that he could see, see, see,
Was the bottom of the deep blue sea, sea, sea!

Ickle ockle, blue bockle,
Fishes in the sea,
If you want a pretty maid,
Please choose me.

Oh, we can play on the big bass drum,
And this is the music to it;
BOOM, BOOM, BOOM goes the big bass drum,
And that's the way we do it.

Oh, we can play on the triangle,
And this is the music to it;
TING, TING, TING goes the triangle,
And that's the way we do it.

Oh, we can play on the castanets,
And this is the music to it;
CLACK, CLACK, CLACK go the castanets,
And that's the way we do it.

Oranges and lemons,
Say the bells of St Clement's.

You owe me five farthings,
Say the bells of St Martin's.

When will you pay me?
Say the bells of Old Bailey.

When I grow rich,
Say the bells of Shoreditch.

When will that be?
Say the bells of Stepney.

I do not know,
Says the great bell at Bow.

Here comes a candle to light you to bed;
Here comes a chopper to chop off your head!
Chip chop, chip chop, the last man's head.

Puss came dancing out of a barn
With a pair of bagpipes under her arm;
She could sing nothing but, Fiddle-de-dee,
  the mouse has married the bumblebee.
Pipe, cat; dance, mouse;
We'll have a wedding at our good house.

Food

When Jacky's a good boy,
He shall have cakes and custard;
But when he does nothing but cry,
He shall have nothing but mustard.

If you should meet a crocodile,
Don't take a stick and poke him;
Ignore the welcome in his smile,
Be careful not to stroke him.

64

For as he sleeps upon the Nile,
He thinner gets and thinner;
When e'er you meet a crocodile,
He's ready for his dinner.

65

If all the world were paper,
And all the sea were ink,

If all the trees were bread and cheese,
What would we have to drink?

Under the water,

Under the sea,

Catching fishes

For my tea.

Polly put the kettle on,
Polly put the kettle on,
Polly put the kettle on,
We'll all have tea.

Sukey take it off again,
Sukey take it off again,
Sukey take it off again,
They've all gone away.

Pease porridge hot,
Pease porridge cold,
Pease porridge in the pot,
Nine days old;
Some like it hot,
Some like it cold,
Some like it in the pot,
Nine days old.

Half a pound of tuppenny rice,

Half a pound of treacle,

Mix it up and make it nice –

Pop goes the weasel!

71

Higglety, pigglety, pop!

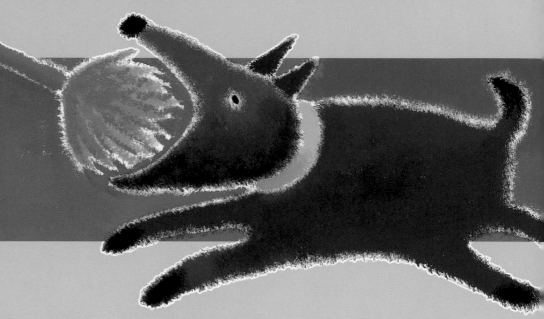

The dog has eaten the mop;

The pig's in a hurry,

The cat's in a flurry,

Higglety, pigglety, pop!

by Samuel Griswold Goodrich

73

Elsie Marley is grown so fine,
She won't get up to feed the swine;
But lies in bed till half past nine,
Lazy Elsie Marley.

Hickety, pickety, my black hen,
She lays eggs for gentlemen;
Gentlemen come every day
To see what my black hen doth lay;
Sometimes nine and sometimes ten,
Hickety, pickety, my black hen.

Charley Barley, butter and eggs,
Sold his wife for three duck eggs;

When the ducks began to lay,
Charley Barley flew away.

Bat, bat, come under
    my hat,
And I'll give you
    a slice of bacon;
And when I bake,
I'll give you a cake,
If I am not mistaken.

Pat-a-cake, pat-a-cake, baker's man,

Bake me a cake as fast as you can;

Pat it and prick it and mark it with B,

Put it in the oven for baby and me.

Sing a song of sixpence,
A pocket full of rye;
Four and twenty blackbirds
Baked in a pie.

When the pie was opened,
The birds began to sing:
Wasn't that a dainty dish
To set before a king?

The king was in his counting-house
Counting out his money;
The queen was in the parlour
Eating bread and honey.

The maid was in the garden
Hanging out the clothes,
When down came a blackbird
And pecked off her nose.

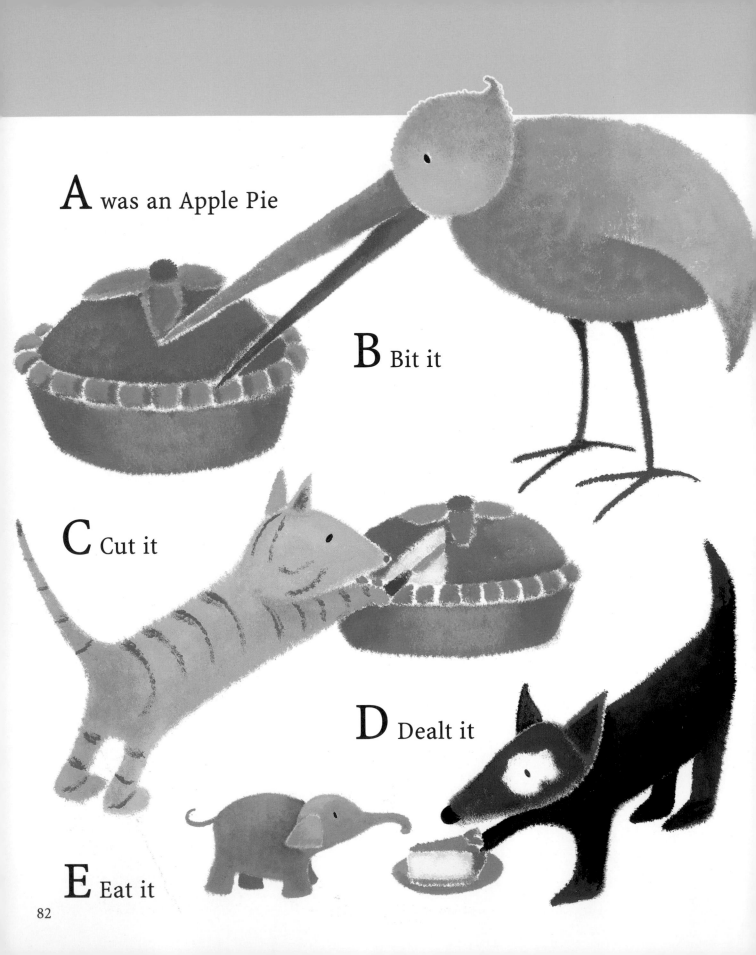

A was an Apple Pie

B Bit it

C Cut it

D Dealt it

E Eat it

F Fought for it

G Got it

H Had it

I Inspected it

J Jumped for it

K Kept it

83

L Longed for it

M Mourned it

N Nodded at it

O Opened it

P Peeped in it

Q Quartered it

R Ran for it

S Stole it

T Took it

U Upset it

V Viewed it

W Wanted it

X, Y, Z and ampersand
All wished for a piece in hand.

Who made the pie?
I did.

Who stole the pie?
He did.

Who found the pie?
She did.

Who ate the pie?
You did.

Who cried for pie?
We all did.
Apple pie, pudding
and pancakes.
All begins with A.

Little Jack Horner,
Sat in the corner,
Eating his Christmas pie;
He put in his thumb,
And pulled out a plum,
And said, What a good boy am I!

The Lion and the Unicorn
Were fighting for the crown;
The Lion beat the Unicorn
All around the town.

Some gave them white bread,
And some gave them brown;
Some gave them plum cake
And sent them out of town.

Handy Pandy, Jack-a-dandy,

Loves plum cake and sugar candy;

He bought some at a grocer's shop,

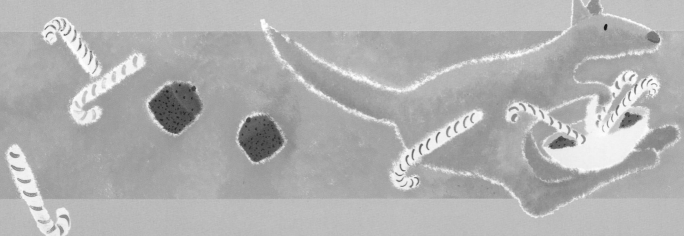

And out he came, hop, hop, hop.

Clap hands for mama till papa come!
Bring cake and sugar plum,
And give baby some!

Purple plums that hang so high,
I shall eat you by and by.

Nature

I'm glad the sky is painted blue,
And the earth is painted green;
With such a lot of nice fresh air
All sandwiched in between.

What is pink?
A rose is pink
By the fountain's brink.

What is red?
A poppy's red
In its barley bed.

What is blue?
The sky is blue
Where the clouds
float through.

What is white?
A swan is white
Sailing in the light.

What is yellow?
   Pears are yellow,
Rich and ripe
   and mellow.

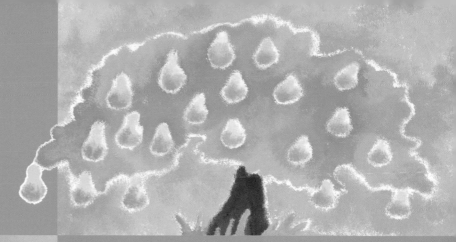

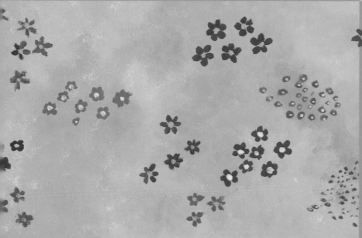

What is green?
   The grass is green,
With small flowers
    between.

What is violet?
   Clouds are violet
In the summer twilight.

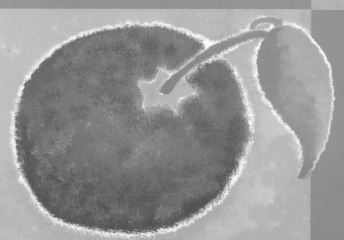

What is orange?
   Why, an orange,
Just an orange!

by Christina Rossetti

I had a little nut tree,
Nothing would it bear
But a silver nutmeg
And a golden pear;
The King of Spain's daughter
Came to visit me,
And all for the sake of my little nut tree;
I skipped over water,
I danced over sea,
And all the birds in the air couldn't catch me.

Mary, Mary, quite contrary,
How does your garden grow?
With silver bells and cockle shells,
And pretty maids all in a row.

Rain, rain,
go away,
Come again
another day.

I hear thunder,
I hear thunder;
Hark, don't you,
Hark, don't you?
Pitter-patter raindrops,
Pitter-patter raindrops;
I'm wet through,
So are you!

I see blue skies,
I see blue skies,
Way up high,
Way up high;
Hurry up the sunshine,
Hurry up the sunshine;
We'll soon dry,
We'll soon dry!

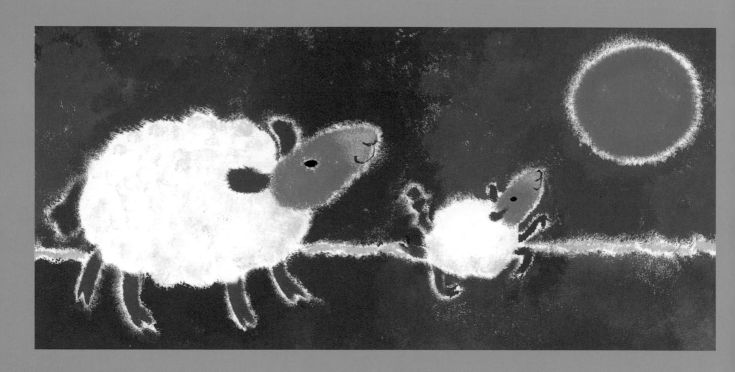

If evening's red
   and morning's grey,
It is the sign of
   a bonny day;

If evening's grey
   and morning's red,
The lamb and the ewe
   will go wet to bed.

Baa, baa, black sheep,
Have you any wool?
Yes, sir, yes, sir,
Three bags full;

One for my master,
And one for my dame,
And one for the little boy
Who lives down the lane.

Four stiff-standers,

Four dilly-danders,

Two lookers, two crookers,

And a wig-wag.

There was a farmer who had a dog,
And Bingo was his name-o;

B-I-N-G-O,

B-I-N-G-O,

And Bingo was his name-o.

I had a cat and the cat pleased me,
I fed my cat by yonder tree;
Cat goes fiddle-i-fee.

I had a hen and the hen pleased me,
I fed my hen by yonder tree;
Hen goes chimmy-chuck, chimmy-chuck,
Cat goes fiddle-i-fee.

I had a duck and the duck pleased me,
I fed my duck by yonder tree;
Duck goes quack, quack,
Hen goes chimmy-chuck, chimmy-chuck,
Cat goes fiddle-i-fee.

I had a goose and the goose pleased me,
I fed my goose by yonder tree;
Goose goes swishy, swashy,
Duck goes quack, quack,
Hen goes chimmy-chuck, chimmy-chuck,
Cat goes fiddle-i-fee.

I had a sheep and the sheep pleased me,
I fed my shcep by yonder tree;
Sheep goes baa, baa,
Goose goes swishy, swashy,
Duck goes quack, quack,
Hen goes chimmy-chuck, chimmy-chuck,
Cat goes fiddle-i-fee.

I had a pig and the pig pleased me,
I fed my pig by yonder tree;
Pig goes griffy, gruffy,
Sheep goes baa, baa,
Goose goes swishy, swashy,
Duck goes quack, quack,
Hen goes chimmy-chuck, chimmy-chuck,
Cat goes fiddle-i-fee.

I had a cow and the cow pleased me,
I fed my cow by yonder tree;
Cow goes moo, moo,
Pig goes griffy, gruffy,
Sheep goes baa, baa,
Goose goes swishy, swashy,
Duck goes quack, quack,
Hen goes chimmy-chuck, chimmy-chuck,
Cat goes fiddle-i-fee.

I had a horse and the horse pleased me,
I fed my horse by yonder tree;
Horse goes neigh, neigh,
Cow goes moo, moo,
Pig goes griffy, gruffy,
Sheep goes baa, baa,
Goose goes swishy, swashy,
Duck goes quack, quack,
Hen goes chimmy-chuck, chimmy-chuck,
Cat goes fiddle-i-fee.

I had a dog and the dog pleased me,
I fed my dog by yonder tree;
Dog goes bow-wow, bow-wow,
Horse goes neigh, neigh,
Cow goes moo, moo,
Pig goes griffy, gruffy,
Sheep goes baa, baa,
Goose goes swishy, swashy,
Duck goes quack, quack,
Hen goes chimmy-chuck, chimmy-chuck,
Cat goes fiddle-i-fee.

If you ever ever **ever ever ever**
If you ever **ever ever** meet a whale,

You must never never **never never never**
You must never **never never** touch its tail;

108

For if you ever ever ever **ever ever ever**
If you ever **ever ever** touch its tail,

You will never never **never never never**
You will never **never never** meet another whale.

One, two, three, four, five,
Once I caught a fish alive;
Six, seven, eight, nine, ten,
Then I let it go again.

Swan swam over the sea,
Swim, swan, swim!
Swan swam back again,
Well swum, swan!

Three grey geese
in a green field grazing;

Grey were the geese and
green was the grazing.

Chook, chook, chook, chook, chook,
Good morning, Mrs Hen,
How many chickens have you got?
Madam, I've got ten.

Four of them arc yellow,
And four of them are brown,
And two of them are speckled red,
The nicest in the town.

Bow-wow, says the dog,

Mew, mew, says the cat,

Grunt, grunt, goes the hog,

And squeak, goes the rat.

Whoo-oo, says the owl,

Caw, caw, says the crow,

Quack, quack, says the duck,

And what cuckoos say, you know

So with cuckoos and owls,
With rats and with dogs,
With ducks and crows,
With cats and with hogs,

A fine song I have made,
To please you, my dear,
And if it's well sung,
'Twill be charming to hear.

Two little dicky birds,
Sitting on a wall,
One named Peter,
One named Paul;
Fly away, Peter!
Fly away, Paul!
Come back, Peter!
Come back, Paul!

A wise old owl lived in an oak,
The more he saw the less he spoke;
The less he spoke the more he heard.
Why aren't we all like that wise old bird?

One for sorrow, two for joy,
Three for a girl and four for a boy,
Five for silver, six for gold,
Seven for a secret never to be told,
Eight for a letter over the sea,
Nine for a lover as true as can be.

119

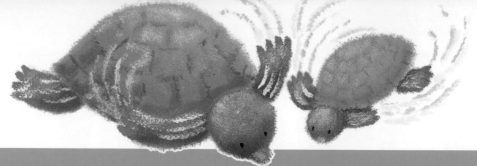

Over in the meadow in the sand in the sun
Lived an old mother turtle and her little turtle one;
Dig, said the mother; *I dig*, said the one,
So they dug all day in the sand in the sun.

Over in the meadow where the stream runs blue
Lived an old mother fish and her little fishes two;
Swim, said the mother; *we swim*, said the two,
So they swam all day where the stream runs blue.

Over in the meadow in a hole in a tree
Lived an old mother owl and her little owls three;
Tu-whoo, said the mother; *tu-whoo*, said the three,
So they tu-whooed all day in a hole in the tree.

Over in the meadow by the old barn door
Lived an old mother rat and her little ratties four;
Gnaw, said the mother; *we gnaw*, said the four,
So they gnawed all day by the old barn door.

Over in the meadow in a snug beehive
Lived an old mother bee and her little bees five;
Buzz, said the mother; *we buzz*, said the five,
So they buzzed all day in a snug beehive.

Over in the meadow in a nest built of sticks
Lived an old mother crow and her little crows six;
Crow, said the mother; *we crow*, said the six,
So they crowed all day in a nest built of sticks.

121

Over in the meadow where the grass grows so even
Lived an old mother frog and her little froggies seven;
Jump, said the mother; *we jump*, said the seven,
So they jumped all day where the grass grows so even.

Over in the meadow by the old mossy gate
Lived an old mother lizard and her little lizards eight;
Bask, said the mother; *we bask*, said the eight,
So they basked all day by the old mossy gate.

Over in the meadow by the old scotch pine
Lived an old mother duck and her little ducks nine;
Quack, said the mother; *we quack*, said the nine,
So they quacked all day by the old scotch pine.

Over in the meadow in a cosy wee den
Lived an old mother beaver and her little beavers ten;
Beaver, said the mother; *we beaver*, said the ten,
So they beavered all day in a cosy wee den.

I know a little squirrel
And his name is Itchy Coo
And he lives in a hole in a tree,
His daddy's name is Mopsy
And his mummy's name is Topsy
And his little baby brother's name
Is Tweedle Deedle Dee;
And they all live together
In a hole in a tree,
Mopsy, Topsy, Itchy Coo and Tweedle Dee;
And all day long
They sing a little song
What a happy family are we.

Travelling

Blue bus bouncing into town,
Bumpety, bumpety up and down.

Blue train rattling down the track,
Chug chug, toot toot, clickety clack.

Blue boat on the ocean deep,
Rocking, rocking fast asleep.

I asked my mother for fifteen cents
To see the elephant jump the fence;
He jumped so high that he touched the sky
And he never came back till the Fourth of July.

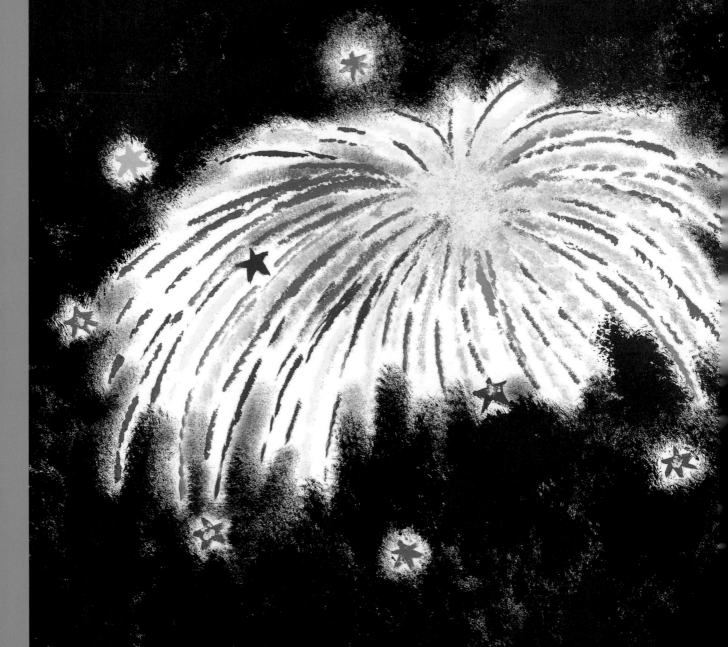

There was an old woman tossed up in a basket,
Nineteen times as high as the moon;
Where was she going I couldn't but ask it,
For in her hand she carried a broom.

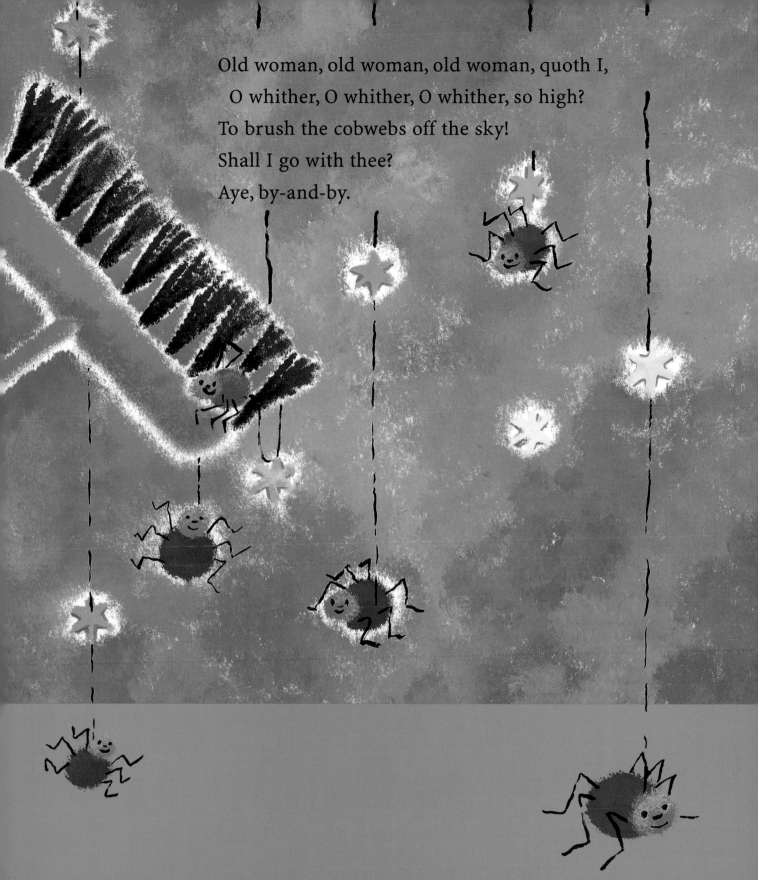

Old woman, old woman, old woman, quoth I,
  O whither, O whither, O whither, so high?
To brush the cobwebs off the sky!
Shall I go with thee?
Aye, by-and-by.

129

What's the news of the day,
Good neighbour, I pray?
They say a balloon
Is gone up to the moon.

Dickery, dickery, dare,
The pig flew up in the air;
The man in brown soon
    brought him down,
Dickery, dickery, dare.

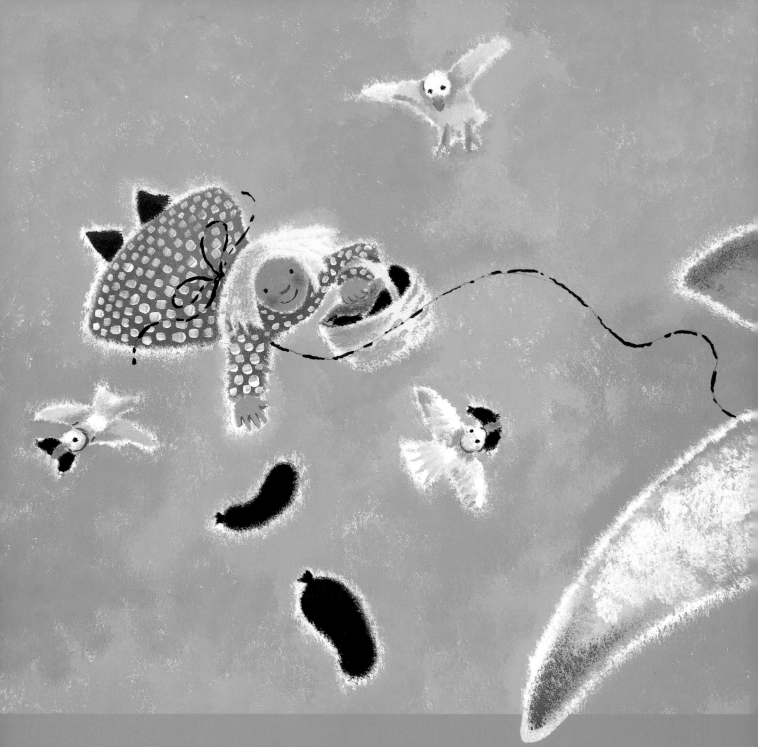

Sing, sing, what shall I sing?
Mary Ann Cotton tied up on a string;
Where? Where? Up in the air,
Selling black puddings a penny a pair.

Old Mother Goose,
When she wanted to wander,
Would ride through the air
On a very fine gander.

Grey goose and gander,
Waft your wings together,
And carry the good king's daughter
Over the one-strand river.

Goosey, goosey gander,
Whither shall I wander?
Upstairs and downstairs
And in my lady's chamber;
There I met an old man
Who would not say his prayers;
I took him by the left leg
And threw him down the stairs.

Three blind mice, see how they run!
They all ran after the farmer's wife,
Who cut off their tails with a carving knife;
Did you ever see such a thing in your life,
As three blind mice?

Three young rats with black felt hats,

Three young ducks with new straw flats,

Three young dogs with curling tails,

Three young cats with demi-veils,

Went out to walk with two young pigs
In satin vests and
    sorrel wigs;

But suddenly it chanced to rain,
And so they all went home again.

Where are you going,
My little cat?

I am going to town
To get me a hat.

What! A hat for a cat!
A cat get a hat!
Who ever saw a cat
    with a hat?

Pussy cat, pussy cat,
   where have you been?
I've been to London
   to look at the queen.
Pussy cat, pussy cat,
   what did you do there?
I frightened a little mouse
   under her chair.

Hickory, dickory, dock,
The mouse ran up the clock;
The clock struck one,
The mouse ran down,
Hickory, dickory, dock.

Bell horses, bell horses,
What time of day?
One o'clock, two o'clock,
Three and away.

143

Ride a cock-horse to Banbury Cross,
To see a fine lady upon a white horse;
With rings on her fingers and bells on her toes,
She shall have music wherever she goes.

This is the way the ladies ride:
Trit-trot, trit-trot, trit-trot!
This is the way the ladies ride:
Trit-trot, trit-trot, trit-trot!

This is the way the gentlemen ride:
Gallopy, gallopy, gallop!
This is the way the gentlemen ride:
Gallopy, gallopy, gallop!

This is the way the old men ride:
Hobbledy-hoy, hobbledy-hoy!
This is the way the old men ride:
Hobbledy-hoy, hobbledy-hoy!
And down into a ditch.

To market, to market, to buy a fat pig,
Home again, home again, jiggety-jig;
To market, to market, to buy a fat hog,
Home again, home again, jiggety-jog.

This little pig went
to market,

This little pig stayed
at home,

This little pig had
roast beef,

This little pig had
none,

And this little pig cried,
Wee-wee-wee-wee-wee,

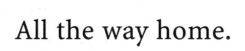

All the way home.

147

Said a frog on a log,
Listen, little bunny,
Will you ride by my side?
Wouldn't that be funny!

148

One leg in front of the other,
One leg in front of the other,

As the little dog travelled
From London to Dover;

And when he came to a stile –
Jump! he went over.

The animals came in
  two by two,
Vive la compagnie!
The centipede with
  the kangaroo,
Vive la compagnie!
One more river, and that's
  the river of Jordan,
One more river, there's
  one more river to cross.

The animals came in
  three by three,
Vive la compagnie!
The elephant on
  the back of the flea,
Vive la compagnie!
One more river, and that's
  the river of Jordan,
One more river, there's
  one more river to cross.

The animals came in
   four by four,
Vive la compagnie!
The camel, he got stuck
   in the door,
Vive la compagnie!
One more river, and that's
   the river of Jordan,
One more river, there's
   one more river to cross.

The animals came in
   five by five,
Vive la compagnie!
Some were dead and
   some were alive,
Vive la compagnie!
One more river, and that's
   the river of Jordan,
One more river, there's
   one more river to cross.

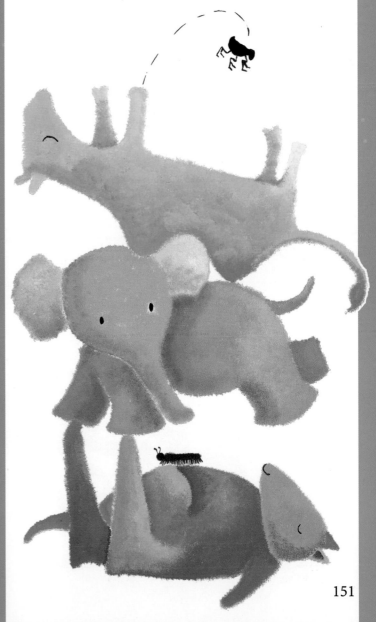

The animals came in
   six by six,
Vive la compagnie!
The monkey, he was up to
   his tricks,
Vive la compagnie!
One more river, and that's
   the river of Jordan,
One more river, there's
   one more river to cross.

The animals came in
   seven by seven,
Vive la compagnie!
Some went to Hell, and
   some went to Heaven,
Vive la compagnie!
One more river, and that's
   the river of Jordan,
One more river, there's
   one more river to cross.

The animals came in
eight by eight,
Vive la compagnie!
The worm was early,
the bird was late,
Vive la compagnie!
One more river, and that's
the river of Jordan,
One more river, there's
one more river to cross.

The animals came in
nine by nine,
Vive la compagnie!
Some had water and
some had wine,
Vive la compagnie!
One more river, and that's
the river of Jordan,
One more river, there's
one more river to cross.

The animals came in
ten by ten,
Vive la compagnie!
If you want more you must
sing it again,
Vive la compagnie!
One more river, and that's
the river of Jordan,
One more river, there's
one more river to cross.

Row, row, row your boat
Gently down the stream;
Merrily, merrily, merrily, merrily
Life is but a dream.

Row, row, row your boat
Gently out to sea;
Merrily, merrily, merrily, merrily
We'll be home for tea.

Row, row, row your boat
Gently on the tide;
Merrily, merrily, merrily, merrily
To the other side.

Row, row, row your boat
Gently back to shore;
Merrily, merrily, merrily, merrily,
Home for tea at four.

The big ship sails through the alley alley oh,
The alley alley oh, the alley alley oh;
The big ship sails through the alley alley oh,
On the last day of September.

Funny People

Indigo Merindigo
Wore a ruby ringdigo,
And danced a highland flingdigo,
Did Indigo Merindigo.

There was an old woman
Who lived in a shoe,

She had so many children
She didn't know what to do;

She gave them some broth
Without any bread;

She scolded them soundly
And put them to bed.

Peter, Peter, pumpkin eater,
Had a wife and couldn't keep her;
He put her in a pumpkin shell,
And there he kept her very well.

Georgie Porgie, pudding and pie,
Kissed the girls and made them cry;

When the boys came out to play,
Georgie Porgie ran away.

Rub-a-dub-dub,
Three men in a tub,

And how do you think
they got there?

The butcher, the baker,
the candlestick-maker,

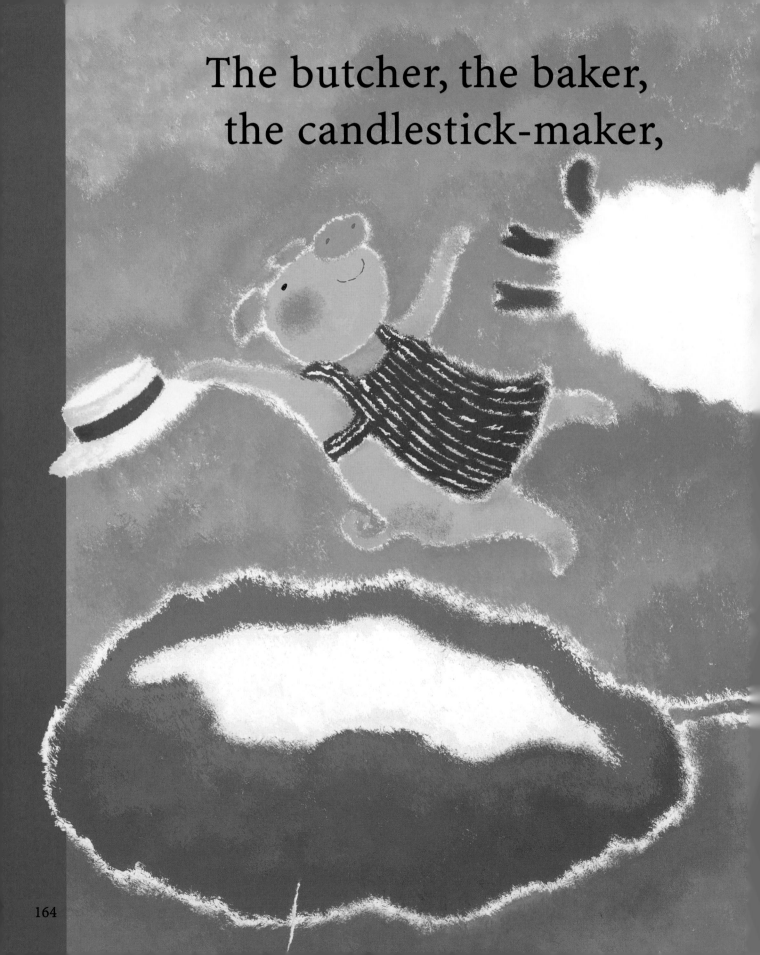

They all jumped out of
a baked potato,

'Twas enough to
make a man stare.

Daddy's in the milk jug,

Mummy's in the cup,

Baby's in the sugar bowl,

We all

jump

up!

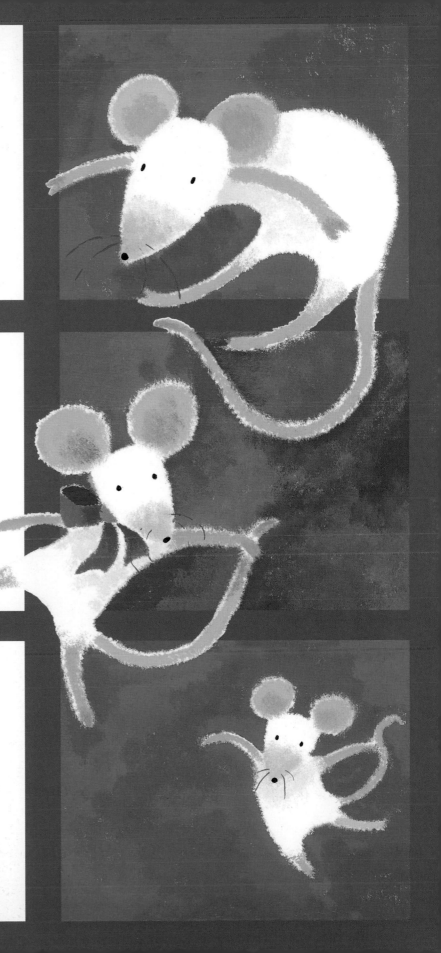

There was a maid
    on Scrabble Hill,
And if not dead,
    she lives there still;
She grew so tall,
    she reached the sky,
And on the moon
    hung clothes to dry.

168

Barber, barber, shave a pig,
How many hairs will make a wig?
Four and twenty, that's enough,
Give the barber a pinch of snuff.

What an odd dame
Mother Bulletout's grown!

She dresses her ducks and
her drakes in cocked hats,

Her hens wear hoop petticoats
made of whalebone,

And she puts little breeches
on all her tom cats.

Old MacDonald had a farm,
E-I-E-I-O!
And on that farm he had some cows,
E-I-E-I-O!

With a moo-moo here, and a moo-moo there,
Here a moo, there a moo,
Everywhere a moo-moo!
Old MacDonald had a farm,
E-I-E-I-O!

Old Mother Hubbard
   went to the cupboard
To get her poor dog a bone;
But when she got there,
The cupboard was bare,
And so the poor dog had none.

174

She went to the barber's
to buy him a wig;
When she came back,
he was dancing a jig.

Oh, you dear, merry Grig!
How nicely you're prancing!
Then she held up the wig,
and he went on dancing.

She went to the fruiterer's
to buy him some fruit;
When she came back,
he was playing the flute.

The dame made a curtsy,
The dog made a bow;
The dame said, Your servant!
The dog said, Bow-wow!

Doctor Foster went to Gloucester
In a shower of rain;
He stepped in a puddle
Right up to his middle,
And never went there again.

One misty, moisty morning,
When cloudy was the weather,
There I met an old man
Clothed all in leather;
Clothed all in leather,
With cap under his chin;
How do you do, and how do you do,
And how do you do, again?

Oh, the grand old Duke of York,
He had ten thousand men;
He marched them up to the top of the hill
And he marched them down again!

When they were up, they were up,
And when they were down, they were down,
And when they were only half-way up,
They were neither up nor down.

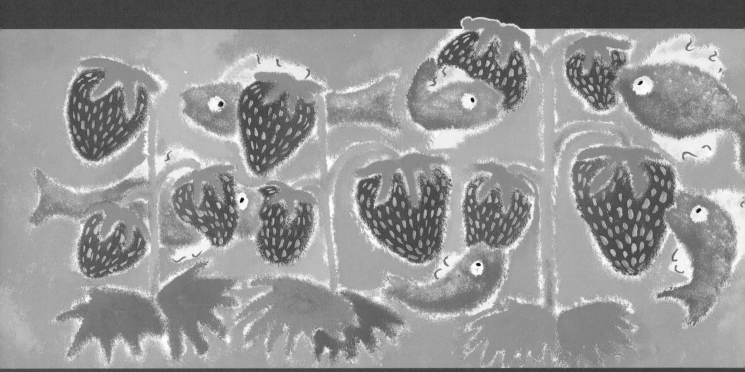

A man in the wilderness said to me,
How many strawberries grow in the sea?
I answered him as I thought good,
As many red herrings as swim in the wood.

Terence McDiddler,
The three-stringed fiddler,
Can charm, if you please,
The fish from the seas.

She sells sea-shells on the sea shore;
The shells that she sells are sea-shells I'm sure.

So if she sells sea-shells on the sea shore,
I'm sure that the shells are sea-shore shells.

Humpty Dumpty sat on a wall,
Humpty Dumpty had a great fall;
All the king's horses and all the
  king's men
Couldn't put Humpty together again.

Bedtime

On a bed of violets,
I lay my babe to sleep;
Above us in the velvet sky,
The stars come out to peep.

Smile down on my baby,
Watch him through the night;
'Til the violet darkness,
Fades to morning light.

Good night,
Sweet repose,
Half the bed
And all the clothes.

Hey, diddle, diddle, the cat and the fiddle,
The cow jumped over the moon;
The little dog laughed to see such fun,
And the dish ran away with the spoon.

The Man in the Moon looked out of the moon,
And this is what he said:

'Tis now that I'm getting up,
All the children are going to bed.

On Saturday night
   I lost my wife,
And where do you think
   I found her?
Up in the moon,
   singing a tune,
And all the stars
   around her.

190

Twinkle, twinkle, little star,
How I wonder what you are!
Up above the world so high,
Like a diamond in the sky.

In the dark blue sky you keep
And often through my curtain peep,
Do you never shut your eye
Till the sun is in the sky.

As your bright and tiny spark
Lights the traveller in the dark,
Though I know not what your are,
Twinkle, twinkle, little star.

by Jane Taylor

191

Star light, star bright,
First star I see tonight,
I wish I may, I wish I might,
Have the wish I wish tonight.

How many miles to Babylon?
Three score and ten.
Can I get there by candlelight?
Yes, and back again.
If your heels are nimble and light,
You may get there by candlelight.

Jack be nimble,
Jack be quick,
Jack jump over
The candle stick.

Riddle:

Little Nancy Etticoat,
With a white petticoat,
And a red nose;
She has no feet or hands,
The longer she stands
The shorter she grows.

Answer: A candle

Wee Willie Winkie
runs through the town,

Upstairs and downstairs
in his nightgown,

196

**Rapping at the window,
crying through the lock,**

**Are the children in their beds,
it's past eight o'clock.**

by William Miller

197

Come, let's to bed,
  says Sleepy-head;
Tarry a while, says Slow;
Put on the pan,
  says Greedy Nan,
Let's sup before we go.

Rock-a-bye, baby, on the tree top,
When the wind blows the cradle will rock;

When the bough breaks the cradle will fall,
Down will come baby, cradle, and all.

199

Listen to the tree bear
Crying in the night;
Crying for his mammy
In the pale moonlight.

What will his mammy do
When she hears him cry?
She'll tuck him in a cocoa-pod
And sing a lullaby.

To my little one's cradle in the night
Comes a new little goat, snowy white;
The goat will trot to the market
While mother her watch will keep
To bring you back raisins and almonds;
Sleep, my little one, sleep.

Go to sleep, baby child,
Go to sleep, my li'l baby.
Hush-a-by, don't you cry
Go to sleep, my li'l baby.
When you wake
You will have

All the pretty li'l horses,
Black and blue, sorrel too,
All the pretty li'l horses,
Black and blue, sorrel too,
All the pretty li'l horses.
Hush-a-by, don't you cry
Go to sleep, my li'l baby.

Hush, little baby,
  don't say a word,
Papa's gonna buy you
  a mocking bird.

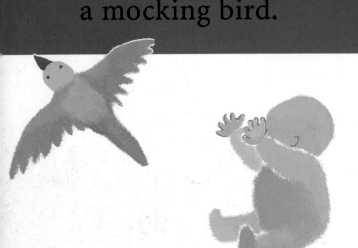

If that mocking bird
  won't sing,
Papa's gonna buy
  you a diamond ring.

If that diamond ring
  is brass,
Papa's gonna buy you
  a looking glass.

If that looking glass
  gets broke,
Papa's gonna buy
  you a billy goat.

If that billy goat
falls over,
Papa's gonna buy you
a dog named Rover.

If that dog named Rover
won't bark,
Papa's gonna buy you
a horse and cart.

If that horse and cart
breaks down,
You still will be the
sweetest baby in town.

Oh, lay still, doggies, since you have laid down,
Stretch away on the big open ground;
Snore aloud, little doggies, and drown the wild sound,

Hi-oo-oo.

That will all go away when the days roll around;
Lay still, little doggies, little doggies, lay still.
Hi-oo, Hi-oo-oo.

Golden slumbers kiss your eyes,
Smiles awake when you rise.
Sleep, pretty babies, do not cry,
And I will sing a lullaby:
Rock them, rock them, lullaby.

by Thomas Dekker

Minnie and Winnie
Slept in a shell.
Sleep, little ladies!
And they slept well.

Pink was the shell within,
Silver without;
Sounds of the great sea
Wandered about.

Sleep, little ladies,
Wake not soon!
Echo on echo
Dies to the moon.

Two bright stars
Peeped into the shell.
'What were they
    dreaming of?
Who can tell?'

Started a green linnet
Out of the croft;
Wake, little ladies,
The sun is aloft!

by Alfred, Lord Tennyson

212

Go to bed late,
Stay very small;

Go to bed early,
Grow very tall.

I see the moon,
And the moon sees me;
God bless the moon,
And God bless me.

Index of First Lines